GUIDE
TO THE
PLANET

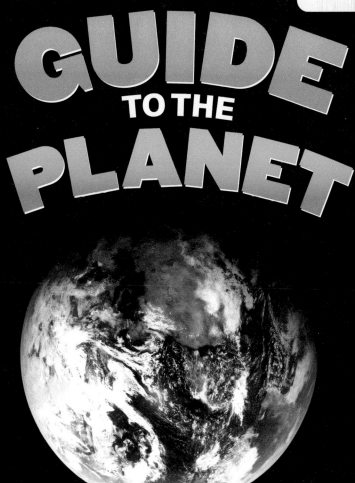

By Matthew Murrie and Steve Murrie

SCHOLASTIC INC.

New York   Toronto   London   Auckland   Sydney
Mexico City   New Delhi   Hong Kong   Buenos Aires

ISBN-13: 978-0-545-10356-5
ISBN-10: 0-545-10356-8

12 11 10 9 8 7 6 5 4 3 2 1   9 10 11 12 13 14/0

Cover design by Michael Massen. Interior design by Theresa Venezia.

Printed in the U.S.A.

First printing, April 2009

♻ Printed on paper containing minimum of 30% post-consumer fiber.

Table of Contents

Introduction

When one sees the Earth from space, it just looks like a bright blue marble against a black background. However, some of the most amazing things in the universe are occurring on our home planet. Many of Earth's incredible facts are stranger than any fiction. Planet Earth is about a world full of amazing places and animals and there are still many waiting to be discovered. This book will take you on a journey to the highest, lowest, hottest, coldest, darkest, brightest, wildest, and windiest locations on Earth. It is a journey that will help you become more in touch with this extraordinary world!

LOOK AROUND

The planet has some incredible features, from a group of waterfalls in South America that can be heard 9 miles (14 km) away during the rainy season to ice caps that are greater than 3 miles (5 km) thick covering Antarctica. The Sahara Desert is larger than the entire United States and is growing bigger each year.

Caves also have phenomenal features. Deer Cave, in Borneo, has the largest underground passage—big enough for a jumbo jet to fly through. Another cave opening, at the Cave of Swallows in Mexico, is deep enough to hold the Empire State Building.

HIGH AND DRY

Below or above ground, Planet Earth is full of fascinating creatures!

Some of the bacteria found in caves can actually "eat" rock. One particular cave bacteria can produce one of the strongest acids known to man, sulfuric acid. Another interesting organism is the cave angelfish, which can actually make its way up the vertical cave walls using microscopic hooks on its fins.

Some organisms have a more straightforward method to conquering their territory: they simply take over all available land. A single locust swarm can cover 463 square miles—the size of Los Angeles, or the island of Okinawa, Japan—and consume everything in its path.

UP IN THE AIR

There are spectacular organisms that inhabit the air around us. In Sarawak, Borneo, three million wrinkle-lipped bats leave their cave each night in search of food. This number is equal to the population of Chicago, Illinois!

The sun-loving Arctic tern squeezes two summers into every year. It lives at the North Polar Regions for half the year, where it takes advantage of the nearly 24 hours of daylight. The bird then migrates to the South Polar Regions, where summer is just beginning!

Another remarkable bird is the cave swiftlet. It is one of only two birds that uses echolocation like bats and dolphins. This ability comes in handy when they have to find their 4-inch (10cm) nest in complete darkness. There's more about cave swiftlets on page 46.

ALL WET

Fascinating creatures inhabit the waters of our Earth as well. The oceans are home to swordfish that can swim as fast as a cheetah can run. Octopuses can change their skin tone to blend in as they move across the ocean floor. Dolphins can use air bubbles to trap the fish they prey upon.

The ocean is also the stage for one of the world's greatest migrations. Millions of fish and marine life travel from the deepest part of the ocean each night to feed on organisms in the shallow waters. After feeding, these creatures retreat to the safety of the deep. Some sea life will travel over 3,280 feet (1000 m) up and down.

Your journey begins when you turn the page to discover more about our extraordinary world. It's an expedition through the Earth's biomes, from tall mountains to the deepest oceans and beyond.

Whole Earth

Have you ever wondered what would happen if another planet crashed into Earth?

Well, the last time it happened, the Moon was formed. The impact of the collision was so strong that a massive amount of the Earth's crust was tossed into space. The Earth's gravitational pull kept it from going too far away and, over time, the lost particles of crust banded together to build the Moon.

Luckily, the planet that slammed into Earth had a liquid-iron core—just like Earth's—which increased the amount of iron in Earth's core. The result was a magnetic field that now surrounds the Earth. This magnetic field helps shield the Earth from solar particles and ultraviolet radiation.

EARTH FACTS!

- Without the Moon's gravity to stabilize the tilt of the Earth, the Earth's poles would roll back and forth. This motion would cause the North Pole to tilt directly toward the Sun, melting the polar ice caps and increasing the overall temperature of the Earth!

PLANET QUIZ

1. The Arctic and Antarctica: Which contains the North Pole and which contains the South Pole?

How far would you go to help a friend in need?

How about feeding them your already eaten food? This is how far African wild dogs will go to take care of the members in their packs. These dogs often regurgitate their food, not only to feed their young pups, but to feed sick or wounded adult pack members.

This is just one example of how important teamwork is. Without working together, these small dogs would have little chance of capturing enough prey to sustain the large number of animals in their African habitat.

DID YOU KNOW?

African wild dogs give birth to their young in abandoned aardvark holes.

EARTH FACTS!

- Impalas are **allogroomers**, which means they groom each other. While **allogrooming** is usually only found in humans and other primates, impalas help keep each other clean and free from ticks by nibbling at the fur on each other's bodies.

- **Lycaon pictus**, or *painted hunting dog*, is the scientific name of the African wild dog. The name is in reference to its wildly colored and patterned coat.

EARTH FACTS!

- By digging **a den the size of a phone booth in the snow**, the polar bear's winter home is *40 degrees F warmer than the outside temperature.*

- **Male caribou** will sometimes fight to the death *for the right to breed with a female.*

What is the longest you have ever gone without eating or drinking?

A couple of hours? One day? How about four months? Male adult emperor penguins do just that each year. Going without food or water might be the easiest part of how they spend their winters. Not only is their home, Antarctica, the coldest and windiest continent on Earth but, for four months of winter, it is also in complete darkness.

Emperor penguins must first trek over 74 miles (119 km) across the Antarctic terrain to their nesting grounds. Once together, the colony of male penguins huddle tightly together in order to protect themselves from temperatures that can drop as low as -128.6° F (-89.2° C).

PLANET QUIZ

1. How much of their lives do emperor penguins spend on land?

ANSWER:
1. None. Their entire lives are spent either in the ocean or on the ice shelves of Antarctica.

Frozen Poles

Have your parents ever told you that you could play outside until it got dark? Well, if they told you this at the North or South Pole, you would have six months to play before you had to come home. Both the Arctic and Antarctic have what is called a "six-month day," when the sun stays out 24 hours a day. When the "six-month day" is over, the "six-month night" begins: for the rest of the year, the Poles fall into complete darkness.

Without sunlight, the Antarctic winter gets incredibly cold. The average winter temperatures in Antarctica drop to -58° F (-50° C). At these temperatures, the surrounding water begins to freeze. Once the big freeze is over, Antarctica will have doubled in size with the addition of more than eight million square miles of new ice.

EARTH FACTS!

- Male Adélie penguins have the ability to produce milk to feed their chicks if the female penguins are away too long.

- Antarctica is so cold that if you throw a cup of boiling water into the air, it will turn into a cloud of ice crystals before it hits the ground.

- The fur of the Arctic fox changes from white in the winter to gray or brown in the summer to blend in with its habitat.

Frozen Poles

Can you imagine an animal so hungry it steals food right out of another animal's mouth?

That is exactly how the South Polar skua prefers to make its meals. If a skua can manage to pester its target enough, it quickly swoops down to eat up whatever meal the bird may have dropped or vomited. Sounds delicious!

The skuas can be quite tenacious when it comes to finding their next meal. A skua will stand for long periods of time over a sick or wounded animal, waiting for it to die in order to eat it. This behavior also makes them scavengers, animals that eat the leftovers of others.

DID YOU KNOW?

The word Arctic comes from the Greek word, Arktos, which means "bear." It refers to the bear constellation, Ursa Major, that hangs in the night sky above this region.

The emperor penguin is the only animal that permanently resides in Antarctica.

POLAR FACTS!

- The Arctic tern is a bird that has the longest migrating distance. It flies back and forth from the Arctic to Antarctica, over 9000 miles, every year. As a result, it spends 75% of its life in continuous sunlight.

- Eider ducks are expert recyclers. When their down feathers fall off, they use them to build their nests.

- Crabeater seals don't actually eat crabs. In fact, there are not any crabs in Antarctica. Instead, they eat krill.

- Beluga, blue, and narwhal whales use their foreheads to bust through ice as they swim through the Arctic waters!

POLAR FACTS!

- A walrus calf is about four feet long and weighs around 140 pounds (63.5 kg) at birth. They must rely on their mothers for food during the first couple of years. Eventually, the calf will grow large enough to eat seals and even small whales!

- If attacked by a flying predator, the sandhill crane will kick at it while in midair to fend it off.

- The ptarmigan has feathers on its toes. These feathers help turn the bird's feet into what resemble snow shoes. As a result, these birds can walk easily across even the softest snow.

- Both male walruses and musk oxen use their tusks and horns, respectively, to establish dominance among their groups. Sometimes, they will even fight to their death.

In order to survive the extremes of the Polar Regions, the animals that live there often turn to each other.

These polar animals excel at teamwork. When a herd of musk oxen is threatened, they quickly form a ring around their young. By the thousands, caribou travel 1,865 miles (3001 km) together in the longest land mammal migration. The wolves that stalk caribou for food will number up to 30 in a single pack just to take down one meal.

Polar animals seek others not only for food and warmth, but as mating partners. The female petrel can be very selective. In order to choose a mate, she will fly a death-defying obstacle course high up into the air, culminating in a risky dive just inches from the rocky cliffs. Once she finds a male brave enough to keep up with her, she has selected her mate.

Sandhill cranes partake in a much safer dance with their mates. Scientists have determined that there are at least five different dances the cranes perform: an upright stretch of their wings, bowing that resembles a waltz, a vertical leap, a vertical toss, and a horizontal head pump.

DID YOU KNOW?

The musk ox must break through thick layers of ice covering the vegetation it needs to eat in order to survive. Luckily, this is no problem for this strong animal: Every time an ox needs to eat, it smashes the ice with a few kicks from its powerful legs!

Forests

The northern tree line forests can be tough environments to live in—just ask the woolly bear moth. During the winter months, its cocoon freezes solid. In the summer, as it thaws out, it eats as much as it can, but it still isn't enough to become a moth!

The caterpillar spins another cocoon to prepare for winter. It takes 12 whole years before the caterpillar is able to emerge from its cocoon as a moth. However, life as a moth is not long—it dies in just a few days.

Life is not only hard for the animals of the northern forests. Since temperatures seldom reach above 50° F (10° C), there are only 30 days a year in the taiga when trees can grow.

DID YOU KNOW?

Despite being so graceful, great owls are big eaters. This owl can eat up to 1/3 of its body weight in a single day—and double that amount when rearing chicks!

FOREST FACTS!

- The pine marten is not a picky eater. In order to survive in the harsh environment, their diet consists of pinecone seeds, fruits, nuts, insects, mice, birds, squirrels, and dead animals. They also hunt animals such as the snowshoe hare and marmot, which are larger than them in size.

- Did you hear that? The great gray owl can flap its wings in complete silence. Maybe that is how it is able to hear mice running below the surface of the snow as it flies above.

- The taiga forest region spans the entire globe, circling through Sweden, Siberia, Alaska, and Canada. Thanks to its large number of trees, it is a leading absorber of carbon dioxide—the number one cause of greenhouse gas.

Every year, a tree slowly forms a new outer layer of wood, just underneath its bark.

This layer is called a ring. Next time you see a tree stump, look closely and you can see the rings for yourself. And if you count the rings, you'll know how many years the tree was alive.

The biggest living organism on Earth is the giant sequoia tree called "General Sherman." It is 272 feet (82 m) tall and has a diameter of 36 feet (11 m) at its base. A few miles away is the tallest living organism, the Stratosphere Giant, located in California's Rockefeller State Park. It towers at 370 feet, 2 inches (113 m).

SOMETHING TO THINK ABOUT

The world's oldest tree, Methuselah, is 4,700 years old. This means it was "born" in the year 2692 BCE, which makes it older than the Egyptian pyramids and Stonehenge!

FOREST FACTS!

- The redwoods in Big Sur, California, experience "reverse transpiration." This means that they collect water from the needles on their branches and transfer it to their roots. They do this in order to take full advantage of the heavy fogs that commonly roll through their habitat.

- The lowest branch on a giant redwood tree is 200 feet (60 m) high. Try climbing that!

FOREST FACTS!

- The pudu is the Earth's smallest deer. It stands only 12 inches (30 cm) high and has antlers that are only 4 inches (10 cm) long.

- Rather than just waiting to be fed, lynx kittens will often help their mother hunt. In areas where hare, a common prey for lynx, are abundant, the kittens will walk side by side with their mother, ready to ambush together.

- The kodkod is a tiny wild cat with a peculiar reputation. Many farmers believe them to be vampires because of the way they eat chickens. Sneaking into henhouses, they will kill more animals than they can eat, leaving a henhouse floor covered in dead chickens with teeth marks on their necks.

PLANET QUIZ

1. What is the largest bird of prey in the world?

2. What does the word "lynx" mean?

ANSWERS:
1. The Eurasian black vulture. It has a wing-span of 8-10 feet. 2. "White" or "to shine"

Have you ever been grounded for a weekend?

Not much fun. Can you imagine being grounded for 17 years? Well, that is the life of a young cicada. Cicada nymphs are born on trees, but they drop to the ground as soon as they're born. They dig below to feed on tree roots and they stay there, underground, for 17 years!

Once they do reemerge, they will have grown to 1.6 inches (4 cm) long — 1000 times larger than the size when they were born. Above ground, the adult cicadas have 10 days to mate and lay eggs before they die. The cicadas are so numerous they create a constant buzz throughout the entire forest.

How far will you go to get something to eat when you are hungry?

Would you be willing to walk 20 miles (32 km)? Would you make a sandwich that weighs five times as much as you do? Would you be able to carry it? A wolverine would and could do all of that and more. Why? Wolverines are exceptional predators and are equally voracious when it comes to hunting and eating.

As a result of the harsh conditions in the northern forests, wolverines have learned to eat as much as they can whenever they can. Sometimes, this requires them to attack animals as large as five times their size. It is not unusual for a wolverine, which stands no more than one foot (30 cm) high and weighs up to only 40 pounds (18 kg), to make a meal out of a reindeer or moose.

While a wolverine is dining on its catch, it makes sure not to leave any food to waste. Its extraordinarily powerful jaws allow it to crack open bones in order to eat the marrow inside. This particular skill comes in handy when dining on the carcasses that have already been picked apart by other scavengers.

DID YOU KNOW?

Wolverines mark their territories using musk produced from a special gland. Another odoriferous animal shares this gland with the wolverine—the skunk!

FOREST FACTS!

- With their natural habitats being destroyed, the langur monkeys have been finding ways to adapt in more urban environments. The monkeys have also become quite skilled at stealing fruit and other foods from unsuspecting residents.

- The langur monkey is considered sacred in India. In fact, they are commonly known as Hanuman lagur. This name is derived from the Hindu, monkey-god, Hanuman. Langur, on the other hand, has little spiritual connotation: it comes from a Hindu word meaning, "long tail."

- Amur leopards are extremely elusive, both in hunting and eating their prey. After stalking and ambushing its prey, an amur leopard will often drag its kill to a hollowed-out tree where it will then store and eat it.

Great Plains

The Great Plains are so wide open, there are few places to hide. This makes speed an essential part of survival. You may already know that the cheetah is fast; it can reach speeds of up to 64 mph (103 kph). Did you know that the massive American bison can chug along at 38 mph (61 kph)? And would you believe that the big, clumsy-looking ostrich can motor at 45 mph (72 kph)?

Just like on a real racetrack, it takes more than raw speed to succeed. Teamwork is essential. Grazing animals would normally make easy prey, but on the plains these animals travel in groups numbering into the hundreds of thousands. Their sheer numbers help to provide protection from predators.

Predators must also cooperate in order to get their next meal. A single lion wouldn't stand a chance against an elephant; so the pride will spread out across elephant trails and wait for the perfect opportunity. Once a lion pounces on a young elephant, the rest must join in on the fray in order to bring it down.

PLAINS FACTS!

- All major rivers in Asia (the Ganges, Brahmaputra, Yellow, Indus, Irrawaddy, and Yangtze) begin in the Tibetan Plateau. Collectively, they provide water for nearly half of the world's population.

- The prairie dogs of North America build underground colonies, like small towns, that can be inhabited by over a million prairie dogs.

- Due to the scarcity of trees on the plains, the burrowing owl often builds its nest underground. Where it builds its nest is only half as strange as what it puts in front of it—cattle or bison dung. Why do they do this? It attracts dung beetles, which they eat; nothing like having your meals delivered to your home!

DID YOU KNOW?

Great Plains are a feature of every continent except Antarctica.

Over 70 million years ago there was a shallow sea covering the North American Great Plains. The seabed collected sediments during the millions of years underwater. Those same sediments now contribute to the fertile soil of the Great Plains.

You probably know that recycling is good for the environment, but the dung beetle takes recycling to a new extreme.

Across the Serengeti Plains, three quarters of all dung is rolled up and buried by dung beetles. Why? First of all, the male beetle will offer a dung ball as a present to a female beetle. What does she do with it? She lays her eggs in it. As if being born in a ball of dung would not be enough to brag to your friends about, the larvae of the beetle use the dung as their first meals—mmm, mmm, yum! What is not eaten goes on to help fertilize the soil. All in all, it is recycling at its best.

PLAINS FACTS!

- A Mongolian gazelle can jump over 6 1/2 feet (2 m) straight up in the air. Horizontally, one of their graceful jumps can thrust them forward over 19 feet (5.8 m).

- Once a herd of Mongolian gazelles reaches its breeding ground, 90 percent of the females in the herd give birth within a four-day period. It is one of nature's few simultaneous births.

- American bison can grow to over six feet (1.8 m) high, 10 feet (3 m) long, and weigh over 2,500 pounds (1134 kg). This makes them North America's largest land mammal.

- Pikas are renowned singers. Not only do males belt out warning alarms, but they also let out a long call, referred to as a "song," to attract females with whom they hope to mate. They are also believed to greet their neighbors with an "eenk" or "ehh-ehh" as they pass each other coming and going from their dwellings. These sounds are believed to be the pika's way of saying, "hello.

PLANET QUIZ

Can the American bison swim?

ANSWER:
Yes! They are actually - in spite of their size and shape - excellent swimmers.

33

The Tibetan Plateau has an average elevation of more than 16,400 feet (5 km).

At 13,000 feet (3.9 km), the amount of oxygen in the air is only 60% of what it is at sea level. It is because of this lack of oxygen that the wild yak has developed supersized lungs. Their lungs are also equipped with a high concentration of red blood cells. As a result, the yak is able to absorb more oxygen from the thin air.

Another unique feature the wild yak has evolved is a sticky substance secreted from their bodies as they sweat. This substance, acting like a super strength hair gel, helps keep the yaks warm by matting their hair together. This entangled hair creates a natural "sweater" for the yaks to wear.

These attributes give them an advantage in their cold, low-oxygen climate.

PLAINS FACTS!

- A baby wildebeest can stand on its own feet six minutes after it is born.

- Unlike most other animals, Tibetan foxes stick with their partners for life. Even when one of the partners dies, the other rarely seeks another companion. They also share the chores around their homes. Both the mother and father fox take turns protecting their children (known as "kits") and take turns babysitting the kits when the other is away.

- At no more than 7 inches (18 cm) high and 21 inches (53 cm) long, the pygmy hog is closer in size to a rabbit than a pig. Pygmy piglets are even small enough to sit in an open hand.

- Asian elephant mothers carry their babies almost two years (22 months) before giving birth.

Deserts

The word desert comes from the Latin word *desertum*, which means "abandoned place." The actual definition of *desert* is any region that receives less than an average of two inches of rainfall a year. When examined with a careful eye, deserts are diverse habitats that take many forms. In fact, their dryness might be one of the only things the deserts of the world have in common.

Unfortunately, deserts might be getting a lot more common in the coming years. While deserts currently make up 1/3 of the Earth's total land surface—about 19.3 million square miles—they are expanding every year. During the last 50 years, the Sahara Desert has grown southward to claim an area the size of Texas.

DESERT FACTS!

- While the temperature of some deserts can vary greatly, when a desert gets hot, it gets hot all over. An air temperature of 122° F (50° C) may seem scorching hot, but it is relatively cool when you consider that the temperature of the sand and rocks can reach up to 167° F (75° C).

- In the largest desert on Earth, the Sahara Desert, only 1400 plant species have been identified.

- In the center of the world's driest desert, the Atacama, there are places where it has not rained for over 400 years.

- Desert sandstorms can generate walls of solid dust up to a mile high.

PLANET QUIZ

1. What is the hottest desert?

2. What is the driest desert?

3. What is the oldest desert?

4. What is the largest desert?

ANSWERS: 1. The Gobi Desert. Covered in snow for two months each year, its temperatures drop to as low as –40° F; although they climb to as high as 104° F in the summer. 2. The Atacama Desert in Chile. It receives only 0.02 - 0.04 inches of rainfall a year. 3. The Namib Desert. It has existed for over 55 million years. 4. The Sahara. At over 3.5 million square miles, it is about equal in size to the United States and makes up around 8% of the land on Earth.

Surviving as a lion can be serious business.

In the struggle for dominance, male lions will sometimes challenge each other in order to take over as the leader of the other's pride. Once establishing dominance over a new pride, one of the first orders of business is for the victorious male to kill all of the lion cubs less than two years of age. In doing so, it allows the new leader to populate the pride with his own offspring. As a result, he is motivated to devote more time and energy to protecting the pride.

PLANET QUIZ

1. How high can the South African Oryx's body temperature get?

2. Which habitat contains more lions, a jungle or a desert?

ANSWERS:
1. 110° F. It can also stop sweating in order to save its water. 2. Desert. Despite being the "king of the jungle," lions live almost everywhere except jungles. Rather than the jungles of a rainforest, lions tend to dwell in deserts, savannahs, plains, open woodlands, and scrub forests.

DESERT FACTS!

- The wild Bactrian camel is able to drink both freshwater and saltwater.

- The dromedary camel can close its nostrils and ears when a sandstorm comes.

- In order to survive the sweltering heat of the Australian Outback, red kangaroos don't just take cover in the shade. They also lick their forearms. By drooling saliva all over their fur, they are able to keep their entire bodies cool thanks to the heat that is drawn away from their bodies as the saliva evaporates.

- Bats are responsible for planting many of the deserts' cacti. By eating the fruit of a cactus, a bat also ingests the plant's seeds. Since a bat is unable to digest the seeds, it scatters the potential for a new cactus every time it releases its droppings across the desert.

- The tristram grackle and the nubian ibex are special friends. The fur of the ibex can get full of insects; luckily, the tristram grackle is a bird with a hearty appetite. This symbiotic relationship allows the bird to eat and the Ibex to live with fewer insects crawling through its fur.

Mountain Heights

Mountains cover 24% of the land surface on Earth. Living conditions in this environment can be very harsh. Above 16,000 ft (4.7 km), air has only half the oxygen it has at sea level. Even though oxygen is sparse, one of the largest mammals, the grizzly bear, makes its winter home on these slopes.

The female grizzly carves a winter den in the snow on the side of a mountain. She avoids the harsh winter by hibernating there for 6 months. During that time, her heart drops to 10 beats a minute and she takes only one breath every 60 seconds. The grizzly mother gives birth and loses up to 40% of her body weight while denning with the cubs. When she emerges from the den in the spring she is hungry, and can eat as many as 2,500 army cutworm moths an hour.

MOUNTAIN FACTS!

- The American mountain goat's hooves have flexible rubbery centers to help grip smooth stones and a hard, sharp edge to catch cracks in rocks.

- Some places in the Rocky Mountains get up to 200 feet (60 m) of snow a year.

The Himalayan Mountains set all kinds of world records: the highest mountain (Mt. Everest), the highest mountain pass, the deepest gorge, and the highest living plants and animals.

The Himalayas stretch 1/10 of the way around the world and can be seen from space.

The mountain range affects the climate of the whole world because of its height and length. It causes the seasonal monsoons on the Indian subcontinent and deserts to form on the opposite side of the range. If you stand at the foothills of the Himalayas, you would be in a jungle dripping in sweat at 86° F (30° C). If you make the 5 mile (8 km) hike up to the mountain heights, you would find the temperature to be as low as -94° F (-70° C) with winds of 100 mph (160 kph). Nowhere else on Earth is there such an enormous vertical rise in temperature in so short a distance.

MOUNTAIN FACTS!

- Great waterfalls of snow are called avalanches. They can travel up to 248 mph (400 kph).

- The Rocky Mountains in the US have over 100,000 avalanches a year.

- Glaciers are the most powerful erosion agents on the Earth.

DID YOU KNOW?

Seven percent of the Earth's fresh water is frozen in mountain glaciers?

If all the glaciers in the world melted, the ocean would rise 230 feet (70 m).

Caves

Have you ever had a cavity in a tooth? The Earth has "cavities" called caves. Though caves can be found in many kinds of rock, most caves are made of a hard rock called limestone. However, limestone has a weakness: it is easily dissolved by carbonic acid, which forms when rainwater combines with carbon dioxide.

Caves are very complex types of cavities. It is believed that there are about 50,000 miles (80,000 km) of explored passages under our feet. That is double the distance around the world at the equator.

UNDERGROUND FACTS!

- Caves are even found along some oceans' rock formations. Fish hide in them during the day and venture out at night to feed.

- A cave in France has the only green stalactites in the world.

- A cave in South Wales, UK, has a pom-pom-shaped stalactite that is submerged in water. If the water level drops, the stalactite will break.

- Sarawak Chamber in Borneo is large enough to hold 40 Boeing 747s.

- The opening to Mexico's Cave of Swallows is deep enough to hold the Empire State Building.

DEFINE IT!

Water that is found in caves is full of minerals. When this water drips from the ceiling, a tiny amount of these minerals will be left behind—on both the ceiling and the cave floor. Over many years, these mineral deposits build into icicle-shaped structures known as stalagmites and stalactites.

Stalactite
A mineral deposit that hangs from a cave ceiling.

Stalagmite
A mineral deposit built up from the floor of a cave.

Caves

Would you eat a bird's nest?

What if it was made of bird saliva? Many people do. Bird's-nest soup is made from the nest of the cave swiftlet. This bird works in the darkness of a cave for 30 days making its nest, using only its stringy saliva as building material.

The white-nest cave swiftlet has to find its very own 1-inch (2.5 cm) nest out of thousands of other swiftlet nests in the complete darkness of a cave. The cave swiftlet has an advantage—it chirps loudly and uses echolocation like bats to find its nest. It is one of two birds that use echolocation (the other is the oilbird of Venezuela).

UNDERGROUND FACTS!

- The chick of the cave swiftlet never sees its parent—the cave it grows up in is pitch-dark.

- The cave swiftlet's first flight is in a completely dark cave. If it hits a wall or crash-lands on the ground, it will probably not become airborne again, as the chick will most likely be eaten by creatures on the cave floor.

- Cave glowworms will eat anything caught in their sticky threads, even their relatives!

Echolocation:
This is a process some animals–like cave swiftlets–use to observe their surroundings. The animal will send out a high-pitched sound. Then it listens to the way that the sound bounces back–the echo–to locate and identify various objects in its environment.

When you think of caves, what animal comes to mind?

Probably bats, right? Even when picturing a cave packed with bats, could you ever imagine that 20 million bats could live in one cave? That is about the number of people living in New York City and Los Angeles combined. Bracken Cave in Texas is home to 20 million bats; and when they leave on their nightly journey, the twilight sky turns black. During the nightly venture, they can eat literally tons of insects; and when they return, drop hundreds of pounds of droppings on the cave floor each night.

One of the most unbelievable sights in a cave could be thousands of tiny lights hanging from the ceiling like the stars of a night sky. The bioluminescent lights are produced by the larva of the cave glowworm in the Mangawhatikau Cave in New Zealand's North Island. The lights are deceptive: hanging down from them are sticky threads that catch flying insects. Insects are irresistibly drawn toward the light and then the glowworm takes its meal. Take the mayfly, for example: while a mayfly's life may not be long to begin with, one born in a cave rarely lives longer than 20 minutes. Once they are born, the first thing they tend to do is check out the shiny lights on the cave ceiling above them.

UNDERGROUND FACTS!

- Can you believe there are organisms called snotties? They can be found hanging from the ceiling of Villa Luz Cave in Mexico. Snotties are made of bacteria that live on hydrogen sulfide and produce sulfuric acid as a waste product. You can probably imagine how they got their name. These slimy formations can grow as much as a centimeter in one day.

Caves

Perhaps the most beautiful cave in the world, Lechuguilla of New Mexico, was not discovered until 1986.

It is also the most protected and restricted cave in the world. The fragile beauty is only open to scientists and those mapping its ever-increasing length, currently at 120 miles (193 km). The cave is under such extreme protection that all who enter must sign a declaration to keep the location of its entrance secret. The cave's ecosystem is so delicate that scientists who enter must eat on plastic sheets and put their bodily wastes into "burrito bags"; a single crumb or foreign substance could introduce a new bacterium that could upset the ecological balance of the cave.

After descending down a large metal tube into Lechuguilla, the first room is the Glacier Bay Cavern, which has a floor that appears to be made of a huge chunk of ice. Many of the passages are completely encrusted with frostlike crystals that appear to be snow. About 1.2 miles (2 km) into the cave, you reach the Chandelier Ballroom, adorned with 20 foot (6 m) crystals hanging from the ceiling.

Freshwater

The amazing Amazon River carries more freshwater than all the top 10 rivers in the world combined. Its river basin drains 1/3 of South America, an area only slightly less than the size of the United States or China. The Amazon is a wild river with no dams or other barriers that obstruct its flow.

Would you be surprised to see dolphins swimming in a river? Boto, or pink river dolphins, live in the Amazon River of Brazil. Botos can weigh up to 220 pounds (100 kg) and reach up to 8 feet (2.5 m) long. They are not the only dolphins that live in rivers—there is the Ganges dolphin, the Indus river dolphin, and the most endangered, the Yangtze river dolphin. In fact, there hasn't been a sighting of a wild Yangtze river dolphin in so long that scientists believe the species may be extinct.

FRESHWATER FACTS!

- The Nile River is the longest river in the world. It travels 4,150 miles (6678 km) through Africa, from Lake Victoria to the Mediterranean Sea.

- The Amazon carries 1/5 of the world's fresh flowing water from the Peruvian Andes to the Atlantic Ocean.

- The world's largest river delta is in the Bay of Bengal, where the Ganges and Brahmaputra rivers empty.

- The world's largest mangrove forest, the Sundarbans, is found around the Bay of Bengal.

- The Colorado River is the most impressive canyon-cutter. It has carved 1000 miles (1600 km) through canyons, including the Grand Canyon, the world's longest canyon.

- The world's deepest canyon is China's Yarlung Tsangpo Gorge, which is 3.7 miles (5.9 km) deep and 28 miles (45 km) wide.

What is the largest lake in the world?

On the surface, that sounds like an easy question, but it depends on several factors. The world's largest lake in surface area is the Caspian Sea in southwest Asia. However, its waters are saline, or salty like the oceans. The largest freshwater lake in surface area is Lake Superior, one of the Great Lakes in North America. The Great Lakes form the largest unbroken collection of fresh water on Earth. But the mother of all lakes is Lake Baikal in eastern Russia, which holds the largest volume of water of all the lakes. The lake is a giant gorge that is deeper than any on land, with a depth of more than a mile (1.6 km) and holds most of the Earth's freshwater.

EXTRAORDINARY RECORDS OF LAKE BAIKAL

- It is believed to be the oldest lake, at 25–30 million years old.

- It is home to the only freshwater seal, the Nerpa.

- It is the deepest lake, with a depth of over a mile.

- It is expanding at ¾ inch (2 cm) a year.

- It has sediment at the bottom that is more than 3 miles (5 km) thick.

- The depth from the surface to the bedrock bottom is 5.6 miles (9 km), almost 7 times deeper than the Grand Canyon.

FRESHWATER FACTS!
(LAKE BAIKAL)

- During the winter, the frozen Lake Baikal is used as a highway and can support the weight of 2 ton trucks.

- Deep-water giant flatworms live more than a 1/2 mile (1km) below the lake surface. They can grow up to 16 inches (14 cm) long and eat whole fish.

- Do you think it is possible for an animal to melt? Lake Baikal has one that does. It is called Golomyanka, or oil fish, and lives at the depth of 4590 feet (1399 m). This fish's body is kept in solid form by the tremendous pressure of where it lives. However, when it is brought to the surface there is less pressure and the solid fish begins to melt.

- Scientists have found hydrothermal vents at the bottom of the lake. Before this discovery, hydrothermal vents had only been found in the deep oceans.

Lake Malawi, in East Africa's Rift Valley, has a greater diversity of fish than any other lake in the world.

It has over 850 different species of cichlids alone.

Lake Malawi also has a phantom. It is not a ghost or a superhero, but the larva of the Lake Fly, also known as the phantom midge. At night, they sneak up to the surface and feed on plankton. After feeding, they escape back to the depths before getting caught by predators.

Early explorers thought the lake was on fire because of the orange "smoke" they saw rising from the surface. The "smoke" was in fact millions and millions of phantom midges hatching from their pupa stage. These giant orange spiraling tornadoes climbed hundreds of yards into the air.

WETLANDS

The Pantanal of Brazil is the world's largest wetland, covering 50,000 square miles (129, 499 sqk), which is larger than the United Kingdom. For six months a year, the Parana River floods its banks to form the wetland. Brazil also has the Amazon wetland. Other notable wetlands are the Everglades (US), the Okavango (Botswana), and Kakadu (Australia). Wetlands include bogs, marshes, and swamps; and surprisingly enough, they cover 6% of the Earth's surface.

The complicated dance between predator and prey plays out all over these wetlands. Schools of Pacu and Piraputanga will follow Brown Capuchin monkeys from tree to tree, waiting for them to drop fruit. These fish cause a stirring in the water when they go after the fruit and this alerts the Dorado catfish, also known as the river tiger. The river tigers are the largest predatory fish and get their name from their sharp teeth and strong jaws. The dreaded red-bellied piranhas then come along to eat the leftovers of the river tiger. The piranhas can strip a fish to the bone in just a few minutes.

FRESHWATER FACTS!

- When the rain returns to the Pantanal, fish eggs lying dormant in the soil will hatch out like seeds.

- The Victoria Giant water lilies grow over 6 feet (1.8 m) across in the Pantanal.

- Over 300 exotic-looking fish inhabit the gentle waters of the Pantanal.

- Snorkeling in the Pantanal is like being in a giant tropical aquarium. Over 300 exotic-looking fish inhabit these gentle waters.

Rainforests

THE GREENHOUSE OF THE EARTH

Tropical rainforests are the world's greenhouses. The daily rainfall and 12 hours of sunlight provides these areas with ideal growing conditions. The tropical rainforests of the world cover only 3% of the surface, but are host to more than half of all the plant and animal species.

Not all rainforests are alike; there are 5 basic categories:

The **lowland tropical forest** covers 2/3 of the total rainforest area and grows at elevations up to 3,280 feet (1,000 m). The Amazon rainforest is a lowland tropical forest along with the Zaire River basin, Central American, West African, and Southeast Asian rainforests.

Rainforests

Tropical deciduous forests are found in areas a few degrees north and south of the equator. The climate there has drier months with periods of heavy rain. About 1/3 of the trees are deciduous and will lose their leaves each year. These forests are found in Indonesia, Africa, and South America.

Flooded forests, or swamp forests, lie near the banks of large, tropical rivers. These rivers rise and fall each year where the trees are submerged, which invariably stunts their growth. South America and Papua New Guinea also have many flooded forests.

Mangrove forests have adapted to life in salty tidal water environments. The trees have breathing roots that stick out of the mud to absorb more oxygen. These forests are situated in West Africa, Central America, and the Ganges delta.

Above 3,280 feet (1,000 m), the **tropical mountain forests** consist of smaller trees, 50-100 feet (15-30 m) high. These forests can be called cloudforests because their cold temperatures bring in a cool mist, which will cover the forest from time to time. These forests are located in Southeast Asia and Central America.

PLANET QUIZ

1. Which are smaller: male or female forest elephants?

2. True or False: Chimpanzee and human DNA is 98% identical.

ANSWERS:
1. Female. Males grow to 11–13 feet (3.4–3.9 m), while females can be as small as 6–8.5 feet (1.8–2.6 m). 2. True!

PREDATORY INTENT

Nearly every jungle predator is an _insectivore_, or an animal that eats insects. Every rainforest–animal group has some insectivore members, mainly because there are so many insects in the rainforest. In the canopy of the Amazon rainforest, the tree anteater feeds on nests of termites and ants. The thick fur of the anteater protects it from the vicious bite of the ants. One mammal, the pangolins of Africa and Asia, has "armor plates" that protect it when it is consuming ants.

Army and driver ants march in groups of hundreds of thousands across the forest floor devouring almost anything in their path, including larger insects, birds and lizards. The forest floor is bare for weeks after an ant colony passes through.

The rainforest environment allows some invertebrates to reach sizes at which they will attack vertebrates. The tarantulas of South America can grow to have leg spans as wide as 10 inches (25 cm)—large enough to eat treefrogs and birds.

One common denominator in each major rainforest area is at least one large, magnificent eagle at the top of the food chain. The harpy eagle in South America, the monkey-eating eagle of the Philippines, and the crowned hawk eagle of Africa have all become specialized in preying on forest monkeys.

RAINFOREST FACTS!

- Caterpillars of the birdwing butterfly intentionally eat poisonous plants and store the toxins, which in turn keeps predators from eating them.

- The blue bird of paradise is the only bird of paradise that hangs upside-down during its mating display. And unlike most other birds of paradise, it tends to perform these displays alone, rather than in a large group.

- The tufted capuchin monkey figured out how to use tools in the wild: They use rocks to crack open nuts!

Shallow Seas

WHERE ARE THEY?

How far can you walk out into the ocean and not drop off into the deep dark ocean depths? In some places, like the western coast of South America, it would only be a 1/2 mile (1 km) or about 9 football fields. The longest walk to the ocean depths is 466 miles (750 k); however, you would not want to make this trip as this coast is off of Siberia and it's most likely covered with ice!

The shallow seas cover only 8% of the ocean floor but are rich in fish and other sea life. The variety and abundance of living things in the shallow seas depend greatly on the two most important factors: sunlight and obtainable nutrients. One without the other is insufficient for an abundance of living organisms. There are many places that receive lots of sunlight but few nutrients, and very little life is supported there. There are also places that have plenty of nutrients but little or no sunlight and almost no life can survive.

DID YOU KNOW?

Algae fields can grow to be the size of the Amazon rainforest.

Algae provides 75% of all oxygen in the atmosphere.

THE WARM SHALLOWS

Would you get tired of eating if you ate 24 hours a day?

That's what coral polyps do; they eat 24/7. Even the biggest coral reefs are made of these tiny sea creatures, each one just a fraction of an inch long. Of course, that means there are billions of polyps in a coral reef. With this insatiable appetite, it's a good thing that these environments are so friendly to life. Inch for inch, the coral reefs produce more food than an entire tropical rainforest.

Corals have developed a symbiotic, or mutually beneficial, relationship with photosynthetic algae (zooanthellae) living in their tissues. Coral are incredible recyclers—they even pass their waste to the algae rather than into the sea, which helps keep the surrounding waters crystal clear. Corals like clear water, so they are never near rivers that empty sediment into the sea or below 164 feet (20 m), where sunlight can not reach them.

These coral reef habitats support some of the sea's most fascinating creatures, including eels, sea snakes, starfish, sea urchins, as well as countless types of fish and crustaceans.

TEN FACTS ABOUT SEA SNAKES

Sea snakes are some of the most interesting predators of the coral reef. Here are some fast facts about these fascinating creatures:

- They can stay submerged for nearly 2 hours.
- They have flat bodies.
- They have nostril valves that close to keep out seawater.
- They have a paddle-shaped tail for better swimming.
- They have lungs that run the length of their bodies.
- They can hunt in packs of 20 to 30.
- They can work together with predatory fish to catch other fish.
- They have the most deadly venom of all snakes.
- Some lay eggs on land.
- Their young can sometimes be born in the ocean.

The longest coral reef is along the coast of the Red Sea, which is 2,500 miles (4,000 km) long.

The largest coral reef in area is the Great Barrier Reef off the east coast of Australia. It covers a total area of 86,874 sq. miles (225,002 sq k), which is comparable in size to the state of Minnesota.

EXTRAORDINARY RECORDS

The coral reef with the most diversity in fish species is the Raja Ampat Islands of Papua New Guinea, with more than 3,000 species. By comparison Hawaii has only 500 known species of fish.

The Raja Ampat Islands have 465 different species of coral. There are only 65 different species of coral in the entire Caribbean Sea.

The Red Sea is one of the most remarkable places on Earth, and is home to the longest coral reef in the world.

Under the surface are an astounding number of colors and patterns of marine life. The Red Sea is exceptionally rich in soft coral, which have a wide range of vivid colors, from light pink pastels to deep dark purples. The sea has thousands of goldfishlike anthias that are constantly swimming, giving the appearance of an orange cloud.

SEA FACTS!

- Not all coral reefs are near the shore. A number of coral reefs, called atolls, surround ancient volcanoes in the middle of the ocean.

- The Great Barrier Reef is made up of over 2,000 individual reefs.

- The Great Barrier Reef is so large, it can be seen from the Moon.

- Dolphins sometimes catch a wave and surf when hunting; they can hydroplane on the beach to catch fish that try to escape by going into water less than a foot (0.3 m) deep.

- Male pygmy sea horses headbutt each other to defend their territory.

- The smallest sea horse is 0.8 inches (2 cm) long and is camouflaged to blend in with the coral it inhabits.

THE SEASONAL SEAS

Would you believe that some seas have four seasons just like on land?

These types of seas are referred to as seasonal seas as they are located in the temperate latitudes of the Earth. They are called seasonal seas because of the periodic changes that occur in a yearly cycle. The changes are not as obvious as the leaves turning colors or snow falling and therefore they go unnoticed by most people.

You may think that ocean storms are harmful to the ocean, but the opposite is true. The storms and strong winds in the temperate zones stir up nutrients from the deep ocean bottom to fertilize the phytoplankton. This process, called upwelling, occurs every spring. Those nutrients, combined with the increasing amount of sunlight, provide a very rich environment. In the summer, daylight can last up to 20 hours, which increases the amount of photosynthesis. At that time of year, the right conditions can produce more food than all of the other shallow seas.

By mid-summer, all the nutrients are used up and the food chain is no longer sustainable. In autumn, most of the food is gone and the remaining animals migrate down to deeper water or toward the equator's warmer waters to feed.

AMAZING NUMBERS

120 = Gallons (454 l) of milk a humpback whale calf will gulp each day for the first 5 months of its life.

3720 = The distance in miles (5987 km) the humpback whales travel to the polar regions in the summer.

13-16 = The length in feet (4-5 m) of a newborn humpback.

2,000,000 = The tons of krill that can be found in a single swarm.

9,321 = The number of miles (15,000 km) the shearwater bird will travel to eat fish in the Aleutians Islands in the Northern Pacific Ocean.

Photosynthesis
The process by which plants capture energy from sunlight in order to convert water, carbon dioxide, and minerals into food (carbohydrates, or sugars). This process occurs in all green plants.

PLANET QUIZ

Humpback whales migrate to colder waters every year. Do they head to the North Pole or the South Pole?

ANSWER:
Both! Some whales swim toward the Artic, while others go to the Antarctic.

DID YOU KNOW?

An acre of kelp forest can produce as much food as an acre of tropical rainforest.

Kelps do not have roots. Instead they have holdfasts, which are rootlike structures that are cemented to the rocky ocean floor.

Can you imagine a jellyfish that weighs more than a ton? This heavyweight is the Lion's Mane jellyfish found off the coast of Scotland. This ocean giant can be up to 8 feet in diameter with tentacles up to 165 feet (50 m) long.

Starfish use their arms to taste their prey.

Picture yourself wandering in and out of giant trees in the tropical rainforest, and then realizing that you are not in the rainforest but a kelp forest under the sea.

Off the coast of California is where the kelp forest can be found. It contains the world's largest seaweed, the giant kelp, which can reach a height of up to 200 feet (60 m). Kelp species are found all over the world, but all of them prefer the cool temperate waters of the shallow seas. You might come across fish and invertebrates feeding and hiding among the kelp fronds or leaves. You might even see a kelp-curler, an amphipod that makes its home by curling a kelp frond and weaving it together with "silk" strands it can create, similar to the way a spider weaves a web.

The shallow seas are also home to many interesting animals and animal behaviors. Dolphins have learned a special trick for finding fish. They jump out of the water to see if they can find birds diving into the water to catch fish. Then they know where to go to find food.

AMAZING NUMBERS

1,500 = The square miles (3885 sq km) of an underwater seagrass meadow in Shark's Bay Australia. This is about 1 million acres, or the size of Rhode Island.

200 = The height in feet that a giant kelp can grow (60 m).

20 = The number of inches the giant kelp can grow in a day (50 cm).

330 = The length in feet the fronds of the giant kelp can grow up to (100 m).

Open Ocean

The deep ocean is the last frontier on Earth. Only one percent of this enormous space has been explored. The deep ocean is difficult to explore mainly because of the water pressure. About 2 miles down into the ocean, the pressure is 300 times greater than at the surface.

Sunlight mostly disappears at the depth of 492 feet, (150 m) but small amounts infiltrate down to 3280 feet (1000 m), in a region known as the twilight zone. The twilight zone is characterized by water temperatures around 41° F (5° C) and extremely small amounts of oxygen. Some animals have adapted to living in these depths. The leatherback turtle's shell is flexible, which allows it to adjust to different pressures. Swordfish have large eyes that permit them to see well in the dark, deep sea. The elephant seal has a thick layer of blubber that keeps it warm in cold seas, and its heart can slow to 6 beats per minute to preserve energy.

ANIMAL DIVING DEPTHS RECORDS CHART

Animal:	Depth:
Leatherback turtle	1640 ft (500 m)
Elephant Seal	4920 ft (1500 m)
Sperm Whale	6560 ft (2000 m)

The open sea has some great deep sea divers.

The sperm whale is probably the deepest diving mammal. Even at 33 feet (10 m) in length it has the ability to dive down 6,500 feet (2,000 m) to hunt the giant squid and other prey.

The "race cars" of the ocean are the 11 species of billfish. The fastest of the group is the sailfish, which can swim as fast as a cheetah can run—a blazing 68 miles per hour (109 kph). The billfish have streamlined, compact bodies without scales, to help reduce friction with the water. They also have powerful "engine" muscles that propel forward.

Fish that are prey find that they cannot outrun predators, so they have developed strategies to "hide." Small fish form "bait balls," which consist of thousands of fish swimming in large circles in harmony. Every fish can hide behind another fish. Larger fish use counter-shading: dark tops and silvery bottoms so they are difficult to see from above or below. Flying fish take to the air when threatened. They can open their pectoral fins and jump to the surface, flying up to 328 feet (100 m) above the surface.

OCEAN RECORDS

- The world's largest fish is the whale shark, which reaches up to 46 feet (14 m) in length.

- The world's largest ray is the manta, with a wingspan of 16 feet (5 m).

- The world's largest nekton-eating whale is the sperm whale.

- The world's largest squid is the giant squid, which reaches up to 33 feet (10 m) long.

DEFINE IT!

Plankton:
Bacteria, plants, or organisms that drift through the seas. These creatures move only on the ocean currents.

Nekton:
Creatures that are able to swim independently of ocean currents, including fish, squid, and shrimp.

OUR WORLD, OUR HOME

From frozen poles to humid rainforests, our extraordinary world is full of astonishing discoveries. The best part is that there's still more to learn about the world around us! But unfortunately, many of these natural wonders are in danger. Habitats are threatened and many animals hover near extinction. We all live on Planet Earth, and it is important to keep learning about the world around us, and to support conservation efforts. See the list below to learn about some things you can do to keep our planet healthy.

- **Bring Your Own Bag.** If you're going shopping, bring your own reusable bags with you. Plastic bags are made from petroleum (aka oil) and paper bags are made from trees. So if you bring your own bag, you won't be wasting either!

- **Don't Leave the Fridge Open.** Try to decide what you want before you open the fridge or freezer door—that way all the cold air won't escape.

- **Down the Tubes.** Turn off the faucet when you're brushing your teeth! You'll save lots of water from going down the drain.

- **Line Dry Your Laundry.** Hang your laundry on an old-fashioned clothesline instead of using an energy-guzzling dryer. You will save lots of energy and you'll lower your parents' electric bill, too!

- **Unplug It.** Unplug all your chargers when you're not using them. Chargers suck up energy even when you're not charging anything, so by pulling the plug, you'll be saving energy.

- **Just Say No to Plastic Water Bottles.** Instead of using disposable plastic water bottles, get a reusable container to bring water with you. Tossing out plastic water bottles creates a huge amount of waste.

- **Reusable Containers Rule.** When it comes to your lunch, the less packaging, the better. Individually wrapped snacks and drinks waste resources. Instead, use reusable containers from home to bring your food to and from school.

- **Ban Styrofoam Products.** Styrofoam never decomposes, making it an environmentally unfriendly choice. Instead of using disposable Styrofoam products, use reusable ones. The Earth will thank you.

- **Put Your Computer to Sleep.** Using a screensaver on your computer uses more energy than if you let it go to sleep. So change the preferences on your computer and give it a rest.

- **Watch Out for E-Waste.** E-waste, or discarded cell phones and computers, is a growing problem. Keep electronics for as long as possible and dispose of them responsibly. You can find an organization that will donate your old electronics to be refurbished.

- **Remember the Three R's.** Reduce. Reuse. Recycle. These are important ways to cut down on consumption and waste.

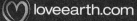 loveearth.com